ANATOLE
IN ITALY

Fondly, for Eleanor N.

Member of the Authors League of America

Library of Congress Cataloging in Publication Data

Titus, Eve.
    Anatole in Italy.

    SUMMARY: Official cheese taster, Anatole the mouse, is sent to Italy to save a cheese factory and discovers a lost masterpiece as well.

    [1. Mice—Stories] I. Galdone, Paul, illus.
II. Title.
PZ7.T543At   [E]   73-3308
ISBN 0-07-064896-4
ISBN 0-07-064899-9 (lib. bdg.)

ANATOLE
IN ITALY

by EVE TITUS

Illustrated
by Paul Galdone

McGRAW-HILL BOOK COMPANY

New York • St. Louis • San Francisco • Düsseldorf • Johannesburg
Kuala Lumpur • London • Mexico • Montreal • New Delhi • Panama
Rio de Janeiro • Singapore • Sydney • Toronto

In all France there was no braver mouse than Anatole,
whose daring deeds were too many to count.

Late at night he worked as Cheese Taster at the Duval Factory,
leaving little signs that told how to make better cheese.
The men never met him, so nobody knew he was only a mouse.

One night there was a letter for Anatole, from M'sieu Duval.
Rolling it up, he bicycled home to the mouse village.

"We're all going to Italy!" he told his dear wife Doucette, and leaned the letter against the piano for his family to read.

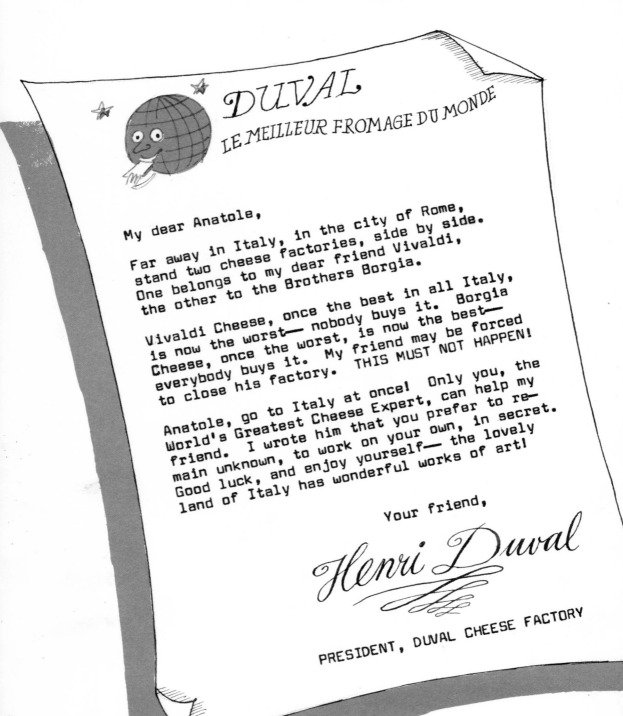

DUVAL,
LE MEILLEUR FROMAGE DU MONDE

My dear Anatole,

Far away in Italy, in the city of Rome, stand two cheese factories, side by side. One belongs to my dear friend Vivaldi, the other to the Brothers Borgia.

Vivaldi Cheese, once the best in all Italy, is now the worst— nobody buys it. Borgia Cheese, once the worst, is now the best— everybody buys it. My friend may be forced to close his factory. THIS MUST NOT HAPPEN!

Anatole, go to Italy at once! Only you, the World's Greatest Cheese Expert, can help my friend. I wrote him that you prefer to remain unknown, to work on your own, in secret. Good luck, and enjoy yourself— the lovely land of Italy has wonderful works of art!

Your friend,

Henri Duval

PRESIDENT, DUVAL CHEESE FACTORY

6

"How exciting!" said Doucette. "I love to travel!"

And the six charming children,
PAUL and PAULETTE,
    CLAUDE and CLAUDETTE,
        and GEORGES and GEORGETTE
asked, "Will we visit new places, and see new faces?"

Anatole nodded. "My good friend Gaston will go, too.
We'll travel by train, hiding so people can't see us.
Pierre the Pigeon will fly on ahead with the news,
and our Italian cousins will meet us when we arrive."

In Gare Lyon, the railway station, the next day,
nobody noticed the nine little mice
who boarded a train and entered an empty compartment.

Perched on a windowsill, noses against the glass,
they saw trees and fields and farms go flying by.
When darkness came they slept, to awake in the city of Rome.

They were met by Cousin Tonio, and also some musical mice,
who invited Anatole to appear with their symphony orchestra.

"Gladly," he replied, "but after I've helped Signor Vivaldi.
Tonight I shall visit his cheese factory."

At the mouse village they met Tonio's wife, Cousin Tessa,
and three small cousins—Marco, Mario, and Marcello.

All the children ran off to Luigi's Carousel, and Tessa said,
"The human children ride up above, on the horses,
our mouselings ride below, hidden under the Roman chariot.
Perhaps Luigi sees them, for we once heard him say to himself,
'People or mice, I like them all, and all deserve some fun.'"

"He's right," said Anatole. "And now I'd like to see Rome."

"By all means," said Tonio. "I, too, am a lover of art."

So they rode around the fair city of Rome all afternoon long,
saw museums and monuments, churches and public squares.
They feasted their eyes on statues and paintings
by Raphael and Michelangelo and Bernini and other masters.

And when they passed the Piazza Navona,
where statues by Bernini adorn the fountain, Anatole exclaimed,
"Ah, Bernini! Of all Italian sculptors, he is my favorite!
Those figures he made from cold, hard marble look so real
that one is tempted to reach out and touch them.
Bernini lived long ago, but the beauty he created lives forever!"

Then back to Tonio's they went, to dine on fine Italian cheese.
Later, riding along crooked, cobblestoned streets,
Tonio led Anatole and Gaston to the Vivaldi Cheese Factory.

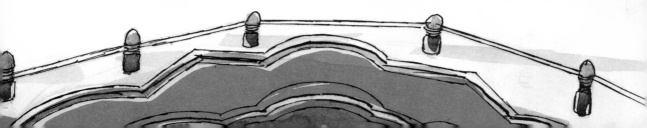

Signor Vivaldi was asleep with his head on his desk,
and even in his dreams his face looked worried.
Around him were piles of orders, all marked CANCELLED.

"Our next stop is the Cheese Mixing Room," declared Anatole.
"We must learn why nobody buys Vivaldi Cheese."

The minute he swallowed some, he knew why. "PFUI!!!
Some dreadful things are in it, things that shouldn't be there.
This doesn't taste like cheese—it tastes like garbage!
We'll go next door to see what Borgia Cheese is like."

There in the Tasting Room Anatole sniffed and tasted cheese—
Toscano, Romano, Pastorella, Provolone, all divinely delicious!
"This I could do forever," said he, "but Vivaldi's in trouble.
Who spoiled his cheese? The Brothers Borgia, perhaps?
Hark! I hear voices down the hall— let's go to the office."

The three brothers, feet on their desks, were talking,
so the three mice hid in a corner and listened.

Said the first brother, "Vivaldi would be surprised to know that the night watchman at his factory is our Uncle Benito, who lets us in late at night to mess up the cheese mixtures. Tonight I dumped some weird things into one of the mixes—SPAGHETTI, SPINACH, and SOAPSUDS! Brothers, what did you add?"

Said the second, "I? RAVIOLI, RAGS, and ROTTEN RAISINS!"

Said the third, "I used PIZZA, PICKLE JUICE, and PURPLE PAINT!"

Said the first, "Remember the night when we sneaked inside, and stole Vivaldi's secret cheese recipes from his safe? That's why Borgia Cheese is now the best in all Italy!"

Said the second, "Why not try to sell our cheese in France, too?"

Said the third, "Duval's is the best there, because of Anatole. We'll ruin Duval, just as we're ruining his friend Vivaldi!"

And all three jumped to their feet and did a happy dance.

"To be a Borgia is to be a villain!" said Anatole angrily.
"They are a disgrace to all Italy, and I must spoil their plans!
Let's leave—perhaps I can think of a way to stop them."

Riding along, they came to Luigi's Carousel, and Tonio said,
"You should see it by day, when it goes 'round and 'round,
with our own little mice, and big children, too,
and Luigi all smiles, so glad they're enjoying the rides."

"The carousel's old, but it's very pretty," said Anatole.
"Just look at that horse in the center, the big blue one!
See the proud head, the wavy tail, the long, graceful legs—
why, it's almost too beautiful to be on a carousel!"

He scurried up to sit on the horse, patting it lovingly.
And as he sat an idea came, and he said sadly, "I have a plan."

"Then why do you look so gloomy?" asked Gaston.

"Alas, *mon ami,* my plan needs the help of the cats of Rome."

"BAH!" scoffed Gaston. "Are you out of your mind?
Who ever heard of cats helping mice? Make another plan!"

Tonio agreed with Gaston, so Anatole slid down, saying,
"Blue Horse, I leave you now, to go to the Vivaldi Factory.
There my brain may have better ideas. *Au 'voir!*"

But at the factory a cat's paw suddenly swooped down,
then stopped in midair as they stood twitching and trembling!

A voice said, "Dear Anatole, do you not know me?
We met in Paris long ago, when I was a kitten. Remember?"

And Anatole, peering at a plump, pretty Persian, *did* remember....

Late one night he had gone to Duval's office to type a memo.
On the desk were two frightened kittens, meowing and meowing.
Their tails were caught in the typewriter roller!

With all his might he had pushed a ruler against the roller,
turning the roller inch by inch 'til the kittens were free.

How thankful they had been! *"Merci, merci, merci!*
We are Babette and Nanette, your friends forevermore!"....

Now he looked at the cat before him. "Then you are Babette?"

"Non, non—Nanette! Babette is back in Paris, with Duval.
I belong to Vivaldi now. Are you here to help my master?"

"I am," said he. "Tell me, do the Roman cats have a leader?"

Nanette nodded. "Each year they choose a Queen of Cats."

"It's important that I meet her—do you ever see your Queen?"

She purred. "I see her whenever I look in my mirror.
I am the Queen of Cats, at your service! What is your wish?"

He told his plan, then said, "Your Highness, I ask only this—
forbid your subjects to enter the Borgia factory tomorrow."

"Granted! I'll send my messengers out at once, Anatole.
Our part is easy, yours difficult and dangerous. Good luck!"

And with a flirt of her fluffy tail, she darted away.

Then Anatole called a meeting of mice, ten thousand strong!
They all crowded into the Vivaldi Cheese Factory.
"Friends! Romans! Cheese Lovers!" he cried, *"Attenzione!"*
Hearing his plan, they all agreed to help, despite the danger,
and marched next door, shouting, "Down with the Borgias!"

The next day, when the brothers and their uncle
unlocked the factory door, they were shocked to see. . . .

mice, MICE, MICE, MICE!!

Young mice and old mice,
shy mice and bold mice,
mice of all sizes,
dressed in disguises,
mice of all shapes
in caps and in capes
were sitting in cheese
'way up to their knees!

There were mice running races,
mice making faces,
mice calling names,
mice playing games—
  tossing chunks of cheese,
  packing trunks with cheese,
  building towers of cheese,
  planting flowers in cheese,
  throwing darts at cheese,
  pushing carts through cheese,
  nailing nails in cheese,
  filling pails with cheese,
  shooting arrows at cheese,
  wheeling barrows through cheese!!!

The Borgias turned red with rage,
    and all started talking at once.

"Every mouse in Rome must be here!"
"Oh, those terrible, terrible mice—
    what have they done to our cheese?"
"What a dreadful, dirty, messy mess—
    who'd buy it now? Not a soul."
"We might have to close our factory!"

    And the men began screaming,
"BE OFF! BEGONE! AWAY WITH YOU!
GET OUT! GET LOST! GET YOU GONE!"

Scream, scream as they might,
    The mice didn't heed them,
But stayed right in sight
    With *Guess-Who* to lead them!

Then the mischievous mice,
    With sly little smiles,
Made fences of cheese
    And jumped over the stiles!

The men turned *purple* with rage, but the mice went merrily on—
prancing, dancing, skipping, tripping, whirling, twirling—
flying kites, having fights, lighting lights in the cheese,
doing kicks, playing tricks, sticking sticks in the cheese—
　　toasting it, roasting it, boiling it, broiling it,
　　taking long hikes in it, riding their bikes in it!

And all the while they ate, ATE, ATE, ATE, ATE!!!

"FETCH MOUSETRAPS!" roared the uncle, and this was done.

But Anatole and the mice played leapfrog over the traps,
hopping so nimbly that not one mouse was caught!

"FETCH BROOMS!" roared the uncle. "WE'LL SQUASH THEM DEAD!"
The four men ran out to the broom closet, and Anatole said,
"Mice, spread soft, sticky cheese on the floor near the door.
Then we'll hide in mouseholes to watch the fun. Hurry!"

The door opened, the Borgias dashed in, and down they fell,
head over heels in the gooey, gluey, gummy mess of cheese!

They tried standing up, but they kept falling down,
slipping and sliding and stumbling, all smeared with cheese!

"Out of the mouseholes!" cried Anatole. "We're ready to march.
Remember to bite their clothes, not their skin! Onward, Mice!"

U.S. 1 81358

At sight of the ten thousand mice marching toward them,
the men staggered to their feet and fled, followed by Anatole.
They ran straight to the police, shouting, "WE GIVE UP!
We spoiled Vivaldi's cheese and stole his secret recipes!"

On the way to prison, the Borgias said, "*Per favore,*
give Signor Vivaldi our factory—it's no use to us now."

Anatole said softly, "Vivaldi is saved—my job is done."

But back at Tonio's, he learned of another job to do.

Tessa said sadly, "Luigi's Carousel is closed. It caught fire, and everything burned but the big blue horse in the center. How he'll miss his carousel, and all the children, too! Having it fixed would cost a lot—he's much too poor. Clever Cousin Anatole, please help this nice, kind man!"

"I am the seventh son of a seventh son," answered Anatole. "Something tells me the big blue horse is not what it seems. We'll ride at midnight—it's time for another good deed!"

When the clock struck twelve, they went to Luigi's Carousel.

There Anatole ordered them to climb the blue horse's head.
Carefully they chipped off the layers of blue paint,
to reveal the true beauty of the horse, in purest white marble.

"Voilà!" cried Anatole. "Behold a statue by the great Bernini!
Many of the master's early works were lost, and this is one.
Beneath the paint I recognized his classic style.
Now we'll hang a sign on the horse, for Luigi to see."

Later that morning they saw an excited Luigi run off, returning with an excited art expert, Salvatore Santini.

Si, si," said Santini, "it *is* a Bernini! All Italy thanks you! We'll pay well for the statue—you'll never be poor again. And it will be called *Luigi's* Bernini, for you found it."

"*Scusi,* Signor, but you are mistaken," said Luigi. "Call it *Anatole's* Bernini—*he* deserves the credit, not I."

"Then Anatole's Bernini it shall be!" said Santini.

The proud mice saluted Anatole, then bowed low before him.

The last few days in Italy were busy, happy ones for Anatole.

He performed the Anatole Concerto with the Roman Mouse Sinfonia,
playing the piano and conducting at the same time,
at three o'clock in the morning, in the ancient Colosseum.
So loud was the applause that the concert was repeated,
at three the next morning, under the ancient Arch of Titus.

(Nanette, Queen of Cats, also applauded Anatole.
So as not to alarm the mice, she sat far back, out of sight.)

The mice gave Anatole a gift, a statue of himself,
beautifully molded of Mozarella cheese.
They said their newest village would be named—*Anatoliano!*

"Grazie, grazie," said he. "Italy has honored me deeply.
This statue I shall keep forever, under glass. *Arrivederci!"*

"BRAVO! BRAVISSIMO!" shouted all the tiny music lovers.
"VIVA ANATOLE, IL MAESTRO MAGNIFICO!!!"

Then the French mice went to the railway station,
for it was train time, time to be leaving Rome for home.

The French and Italian cousins waved in fond farewell
as the train left the great railway station in Rome.

Again they sat on a sill, saw trees and fields and farms fly by.
What with sleeping and waking and waking and sleeping,
at last the little travelers were back in their beloved Paris.

Then Anatole declared, "Truly, in all France,
there are no happier, merrier mice than ourselves,
for although we love Italy dearly,
there is no cheese like French cheese!"

FINIS

o